SWOLE: TRIPLE DROP SETS

Published and written by: Golden Czermak
1st Edition

WARNING: This is a **short story** written for mature readers. It is pure escapism, containing adult themes, coarse language, erotic sexual situations, male-male sex, and nudity.

ACKNOWLEDGEMENTS

Ah the triple drop set, bane of my existence and whose painful after effects are known to me thanks to my friend, RJ Ritchie. Hopefully, you still want to lift with me after reading these stories.

Much love my friend, always.

SWOLE

TRIPLE DROP SETS

CHAPTER 1

THE PROPOSITION

L IKE JONNY, CAMERON DID EVERY day that particular week in March – which masqueraded as spring break to some, but for him was a wholly different experience – he awoke early. It was Thursday morning, his eyes greeting the sunlight that slipped in through narrow gaps in the dark draperies. As he moved around on the guest room's rigid mattress, Jonny's body ached. The stiff springs found all the wrong places and cruelly poked at him. The sensation was familiar, conjuring horrible memories of his Aunt Betty's emaciated pincers, tipped with fuchsia nail polish, poking and nipping at his soft cheeks. Thankfully,

Jonny's mind was reeling and after rubbing his cheeks to feel for scars, he quickly swept the bad memories away.

Other things soon filled the space that was left behind; they were not as thin as bed springs or bony fingers, but just as hard. Those things managed to find all the *right* places on, and even deep inside him, ever since he'd arrived at Trent Cassidy's house the past weekend.

Trent, he thought. The name made all his current aches seem more bearable; pleasurable even.

But there was something else about Trent – distant and dreamlike though a steamy haze – that loitered in Jonny's mind. He thought (and it was damn near laughable that Jonny could have thought such a thing) that just hours ago, beneath a deluge of hot water and slick, soapy suds, he had somehow managed to assume the role of a poker himself, stoking the inner fires of that extremely hot alpha male.

No way did that happen, Jonny thought to himself. *You dreamed up every bit of that shit, thinking you can even hold a candle to someone like Trent. You don't even come close to being as sexy or dominating as someone like him. You never have been and certainly never will…*

Jonny's mouth was quick to spring open, ready to launch a verbal assault against the mean – if not mostly right – part of himself, but then he realized that he didn't have to. As if the action of opening his mouth were enough, the steam that seemed to cloud his memory cleared. He hadn't dreamed it up; it was true. Every sight, every smell, every feel he could recall. All of it.

Admittedly, a part of Jonny *had* fantasized about spreading Trent's cheeks apart with his cock, burrowing himself balls-deep into that tight hole. It started the night Jonny was first lured into Trent's gym, laying those intimidated eyes on that man's amazing ass in the locker rooms. As fate would have it, the persistent daydream that would creep in during quiet moments became a slippery reality last night. Casanova Cassidy himself had let a nerd fuck him and surely that upset the cosmic balance somewhere in the universe.

Oh, come on Jonny, that's a bit of an exaggeration, isn't it? the voice in his head rebuked.

"Ugh," was all Jonny could manage as a response. He scrambled to bury his face in a pillow.

Trent had shifted the balance, the dynamic between the two men changing. If he had been the only player in the game, that change would have been for the better. But life for Jonny was never that simple. There were other pieces on the board that were in motion: classes, work, money (or lack thereof), and the largest of those other pieces was a man named Jared Hughes.

Ah, Jared... Jonny thought reverently, and the flavor of whiskey suddenly tickled the back of his throat.

Jonny had been developing feelings for his close friend as well. The funny thing was he happened to live under the same roof as Trent. Those emotional ties had intensified a hundredfold since Monday nonetheless, fleeting impulses acted upon without much thought in ravenous ways.

What an absolute cluster fuck this is! Jonny's frustration returned. *You really should just stick to playing* World of Warcraft. *At least there you wouldn't keep finding yourself in the middle of so much shit.*

In his mind's eye, he could see Trent standing to one side flexing his big muscles like a gym rat does instinctively upon seeing his reflection in a bathroom mirror. Jared was positioned on the other side, giving Jonny his undivided attention, while grabbing at the front of his overstuffed jeans. What a position to be in: stuck between two hunky men that were lusting after him. Men, he felt, that were well above his league.

Jonny knew that the time for making a final decision was fast approaching. His heart beat anxiously and it felt like a heavy boulder had been placed in the center of his chest. To move forward, he would have to roll it off in one direction, the rock ending his relationship with the unlucky loser that found himself in its path of destruction. The one who wasn't flattened by the weight of this choice would be his, or so he hoped. Forever would be nice, but only time could tell.

All of this hinged on Johnny's ability to make the choice without crushing himself in the process.

Trent… or Jared.

Jared… or Trent.

Trent… or Jared.

Jared… or Trent.

Jonny didn't want to decide; he'd lose out on half of what made this week great.

You're such a selfish asshole… his nagging inner voice began again, but then Trent's words from the night before cut through the negative thoughts like a hot knife through butter.

"I have a proposition for you, but only if you're game…"

"Okay, you have my attention," Jonny recalled himself saying. "What is it that you're proposing?"

Jonny then remembered Trent's eyebrow arching quite high before…

… he backed up to make sure the last streaks of Jonny's cum were rinsed off his back.

"Like I said: I love seeing you happy, Jonny-boy and you *have* opened me up to new things, you little fucker."

"*Big* fucker," Jonny said, but he paused when Trent's dick started to grow again as if to say, 'oh really now?'

Trent's lips curled up slightly into a smirk. He dipped his head beneath the water and it splashed cheerfully around his hair, streams of it rolling down his body. Eventually they caressed his long shaft, coating it with a silky luster. It was nearly full again.

"Like I was saying," Trent said while squatting to pick up the bar of soap which had fallen to the tile floor. As he smoothed the dented corner with his thumb, his dick seemed to wave. "I know what makes you happy and I might not like all of those the things, but the fact you are happy in the end makes it worthwhile."

Does he realize how torn I am? Jonny thought as Trent stood. His dick certainly looked capable of tearing things up.

The big man soaped up his palms before grabbing hold of his shaft with them. Then, he squeezed tightly. Suds oozed out between his fingers and he started to stroke himself, casually speaking the entire time.

"So, I propose that *both* you and J-rod join me tonight here in Swole."

Jonny felt a spark, but it wasn't a pleasant one. He was positive his face looked like he was having a stroke, or that his brain had otherwise short-circuited.

Trent appeared unfazed. His dick grew even harder.

"W-what d-did you say?" Jonny stuttered.

"You suddenly go deaf?"

Trent's self-fondling continued.

"N-no… b-but Jesus, Trent. What on Earth makes you think Jared would be remotely interested in doing something like that? You know as well as I do: he won't come and will probably tell me to fuck off without so much as a second thought."

Jonny grew confident, sure that he was right. You didn't have to look very hard to see that Jared had zero interest being near Trent, never mind wanting to *do* anything sexual.

"If J-rod does," Trent said, "then you're stuck with me, which isn't that bad a situation to be in. But trust me. He will come. You leave on Saturday morning, right?"

The question made Jonny feel more anxious. There were just two days left.

"Yeah," he replied suspiciously. "I'm on the six o'clock bus to Marshall."

"Back home to classes, work, and normal life," Trent said. "Waiting for you with open arms."

It was Jonny's turn to cock his eyebrow, though he still felt on edge.

"Yeah, but what does that have to do with any –"

"I still owe you two more workouts to complete the week."

Jonny nodded presently. They still hadn't worked out arms or shoulders. He knew that he didn't *have* to come back to Swole if he didn't want to, but there was a part of him that felt compelled to do so. It was a weird feeling, like Jonny had lost his own sense of control, and Trent's unrelenting double fist-pounding right there in front of him was likely the cause. Precum began to collect at the tip of Jonny's dick's head, a physical manifestation of the fact he couldn't say no.

"Well, *I'm* making a sacrifice inviting him here," Trent said, his dick frothy. "Hell, I'll even let my Jonny-boy decide what gets to happen. It's only fair that ol' J-rod stuff his pride where the sun doesn't shine and make some sacrifices of his own to keep his precious Jonny happy. Am I right?"

Jonny bobbed his head like a puppet and a fat drop of precum fell to the wet floor, getting lost in its wet, blue-gray polish.

"Be sure to tell him about my offer later this morning."

Jonny was still nodding, words too disjointed to come out in sentences.

"It'll be shoulders tonight," Trent said, glancing from one of his to the other. A glob of liquid pooled at the tip of his dick, then spilled over in a thick stream. "It's normally a fast workout day, which will leave us with plenty of extra time. We could make the most of it, if he's game."

"I don't know if he is or not," Jonny replied, his voice soft and innocent, unlike the man in front of him.

"All you have to do is ask. Can you do that for me?"

Jonny gulped. He didn't want to, but knew he had to. There shouldn't be any harm in asking the question at least. He nodded.

Trent released his cock, throbbing and swollen, and extended the index fingers of both hands. He pointed them down toward it while saying, "Good boy. Now with that out of the way, Jonny-boy, it's time to let my man here have *his* fun. Turn around. Now."

Jonny could see himself turning around and back in the guest room, his asshole contracted like a hand recoiling from a hot stove. Trent plus *Dial* soap stung like a motherfucker.

Next time, use Dove, Jonny thought. He let out a little chuckle just as there was a knock on the door.

"Hey Jonny." It was Jared. "I got your text message from earlier saying we needed to talk. Is everything okay?"

Jonny answered with some vague reply as he got up from the futon. Everything was okay right then and there, but he had no idea if it would be after he delivered Trent's message.

"TRENT HAS TO BE ON drugs!" Jared exclaimed, spinning away from Jonny at breakneck speed. His hands shot out, latching onto the balcony rail. They were soon wringing it.

"So that's a no?" Jonny asked sheepishly, the morning air cold on his skin.

"You're fucking right it's a no! There's no way I'm ever stepping into that place, Jonny, never mind letting Trent's egotistical ass try to dominate me. I would seriously punch that goddamn smug face of his if he tried."

The look on Jared's face was angry, made worse by his heavy breathing, creased forehead, and rough tufts of morning hair. He resembled a werewolf about to transform.

Heat started to build behind Jonny's ears, shielding him against the increasing wind. The sensation began prickling like acid down his shoulders. It was miserable, and he was sure Jared was on the verge of telling him to get out of the house.

"Go back to your fucking miserable life in Marshall!" he imagined Jared saying. *"I don't ever want to see you again!"*

The breeze felt cool again, Jonny hoping Trent would come barging in through the French doors like some twisted knight in shining armor (or, more likely, a jock strap) to save him. At the same time, he was glad the musclebound lout was nowhere around. Jared was sour and could have spit venom.

"I'm sorry I asked," Jonny said.

Jared looked unchanged.

Then, unexpectedly, a question leaped out of Jonny's mouth like a fish slipping from a fisherman's hands.

"If you and Trent hate each other so much, why the hell do you live in this house?" Jonny bit into his index finger, expecting a torrent of hateful words to be catapulted his way.

It was a valid question, though. The two roommates were always arguing and giving each other shit. Jonny supposed Jared would be much happier away from all of this, since finishing college and bettering himself appeared to be high priorities. Yet, he stayed.

Jared let out a prolonged sigh, glancing over in Jonny's direction. It was like he was staring into him. His blue eyes were no longer sharp and crystalline, but soft like the spring sky remain for the rest of the week.

"The reason I stay here is because the house is mine."

Jonny sank into his chair, saying, "I thought that Trent owned this place?"

Jared shrugged casually and what looked like a nod jiggled his head.

"Trent and I have a history," Jared continued in a melancholy voice. "We are… were… partners you see."

"*Business* partners, right?" Jonny asked, knowing better but needing to hear it for himself.

Jared laughed, sniffled, then licked his lips. Taking his arms off the rail, he crossed them over his broad chest and let out another sigh.

"Yeah, the relationship business."

CHAPTER 2

CASSIDY AND HUGHES

JONNY SUPPOSED SOMEWHERE IN THE back of his mind that he knew about Trent and Jared. He must have just glossed over the finer details, not that they were any of his business.

Jared unfurled his arms; there were tiny speckles over his forearms like goose flesh.

"Come on," he said, marching toward him then opening the doors. "It's a little brisk this morning. Let me cook up some breakfast for you."

"I'm not all that hungry," Jonny replied, eyes skirting the floor of the balcony. They stopped every now and then, taking great interest in the odd branch or dead leaf.

"I'm sure what I have to tell you is far more interesting than dead tree parts."

Jonny looked up from his seat and before long was standing.

Jared smiled and stepped inside the house where it was much warmer.

"I'll be glad when summer gets here and the mornings aren't so brisk," he said, passing beneath the arch that led into the kitchen. Pointing over toward the bar he told Jonny to take a seat.

"I'd rather keep my hands busy and help," said Jonny.

"Suit yourself," Jared said, walking over to the cabinet where the pots and pans were kept. Opening one of the doors, he pulled out a large copper skillet, supposedly non-stick, but most of the time if you didn't use ample amounts of cooking spray, you'd be left with a burnt mess.

"Snag me one, too?" Jonny asked. "Can be a plain one."

Jared did so with a smile, handing off a large black frying pan. As he did, their fingers brushed against each other and Jonny's cheeks flushed pink when he set the pan down.

"You're so innocent," Jared said, setting his own skillet on the stovetop. Spraying the copper skillet, he told Jonny, "The eggs are on the top shelf, bacon should be in the drawer unless Trent already got a hold of it."

"I'm innocent *most* of the time," Jonny said, plucking the eggs and (thankfully) the bacon from their respective places in the refrigerator. Turning, he closed the door with a gentle backwards kick and took the items over to Jared. Both pans were getting hot.

As the two of them cooked breakfast, the room filled with delicious smells that transported them back to the earlier years of their lives. A time where Mom would be cooking, Dad would be reading the morning newspaper (or in Jared's case the latest copy of *Architecture Weekly*), and they – as kids – would be playing. Now that they were older, both longed for that innocent time again, where others had the worries and they had the freedom to not care about anything other than which crayon would be best to color the drawing of a puppy.

Yet life could only move in one direction, and backward was not it.

"Okay," Jared said over the sizzle of bubbling bacon. "About Trent and I…"

Jonny listened as Jared told him about their history.

It began a couple of years ago, when Trent – then with a much shorter beard and slightly smaller frame – met Jared at Swole's grand opening. Before the rebuild and rebranding, the facility was called The Den, owned by a Charles Wilkerson who was nothing more than a hack job in it for cold, hard cash. The place was known more as a dump than a gym, with its cracked padding, rusted plates where rubber ones weren't used, and cobbled cables. The far nicer services were on the eastern and southern edges of town, the ritzier parts where cold, hard cash did talking as well, just with better results than Wilkerson had done. Those in the north and west, especially students at Logan University with a 'fitness center' far worse than any hotel's, had to travel quite a way to maintain any semblance of a healthy lifestyle, paying premium membership prices for the privilege.

Trent had an entrepreneurial spirit, seeing the potential to make some serious money in the process. Saving his cash over the years, he was finally able to take over the lease and renovate the space, Wilkerson sure to milk him for as much as he could in the process. All of it was a risk, but using his charm (and Jonny was quite sure Jared forgot to say his dick) Trent pulled a few favors for used, old-school equipment. That lured some of the bigger guys in town and along with an affordable membership fee,

Swole proved just what the north side of town needed. Within a year, Trent was expanding into the space next door and setting up the different rooms that had become so familiar to Jonny over the past week.

But back to the grand opening. It was about three o'clock that afternoon when a beastly nineteen-year-old walked in through the doors, catching Trent's wandering eye immediately. The boy wasn't hard to miss by any means; he'd been the size of a bull since his early teens.

"Meat and potatoes never fail the Hughes' boys," Jared's dad used to say, and still did when they met over holidays. He wasn't exaggerating, all four of his boys having good genes while looking great in tight ones all the same.

Three brothers? Jonny thought as Jared rattled off their names. *Oh my God…*

Trent worked his moves on Jared, who was receptive to those advances but aware of what was going on. Trent had a reputation (everyone in town knows him well, remember?) but still, Jared couldn't deny that the man had talent with respect to his craft.

Over time and many workouts, both during and after hours, something seemed to blossom between them like a garden at the end of winter's final frost. Trent didn't like living by himself on the west side of town so much anymore, and Jared, who was trapped in campus housing until the end of his first year, pined for more time alone with this man he was starting to care more about. He didn't want to say love, because he wasn't sure that was what it was nor if Trent could live up to what that word really meant. Regardless, Jared wanted to spend more time around Trent (Jonny knew exactly how he felt) and perhaps learn to change that in him.

"Some things take small steps," Jared's Mom used to tell him, "and though you may feel like progress is slow, any step you can take that moves you forward is a success."

Changing Trent was no easy task, but Jared kept those words in mind and the time eventually came when the two decided to rent a house together. They both signed onto the lease to be able to afford the hillside home. It offered privacy from town and college life, but wasn't so far removed that they'd feel isolated, and others could visit without driving an eternity. The truth was Jared could have signed on by himself, his parents were wealthy enough, but it was a symbolic gesture to him, one that promised happiness for years to come.

Yet, instead of the dream the move should have been, it was more like a bright, fluorescent light shining down on all their imperfections.

Nothing could hide and every crack was exposed, seeming to widen as arguments increased over time. Then, after seven months with no alternatives other than to explode at each other even more, something snapped. The two grew to hate being around each other and Jared poured all his attention on school, moving himself into the upstairs bedroom while Trent, staying in the master suite, focused on running his gym and training his clients.

"Thinking back," Jared said, "I think it was sometime during that first year, waiting on my sentence in the dorms to be over, that I realized Trent wouldn't change. Maybe he couldn't, but overall I was just fooling myself that it was possible."

"I wouldn't beat yourself up too hard over it. Wasn't that around the same time we met?" Jonny asked.

"Yeah, when I was visiting Bonnie," Jared answered, a sparkle in his eyes. "You were there at her birthday party and we started talking."

"If you call talking to the wallpaper a conversation. God, I was such a wallflower."

"Yup, I remember," Jared replied lightly. "It was like you'd been superglued right there and nothing was going to move you. Got you away from the wall eventually, though, didn't I. Jesus, you were sweating buckets on the couch."

"So much that it looked like I'd pissed on the cushions."

"Haha! Yeah, Bonnie asked me later if you were that drunk. I told her no, you were just nervous… and you were extremely cute." Jared found himself looking out across the table. "Wow, I guess that's when I first redirected my lost affections toward you."

Jonny returned the stare, wrapped in gentle affection.

"I think that's why I was sweating so much," he said. "Hindsight twenty-twenty and all. I liked you, Jared. A lot."

"Liked?"

"Still do," Jonny clarified, then looked down to his plate.

He hadn't eaten much food at all, already admitting that he wasn't too hungry before they'd even started cooking. Still, he felt bad about it.

On the other hand, Jared had been shoveling food as he went; he was a meat and potatoes kind of boy after all. Setting down his fork with a clatter, the back of it smeared some golden drops of runny yolk. Jared placed an elbow on the edge of the table, made a fist which caused his forearm to bulge, and rested his cheek against his knuckles.

"Well, there you have it," he said. "The sordid tale of Cassidy and Hughes."

Jonny was using his fork to repeatedly stab the yolk of his over-easy egg.

"So, I need to ask, are you both using me now?"

"Yes." The word came out of Jared's mouth quickly and effortlessly. "J, I think we've been 'using' you to fill the gaps in our personal lives. I *also* think you've been doing the same, using us to fill the one left in your chest by that bastard Fred."

Fred, Jonny thought bitterly; the name was repugnant. *Now there's someone I hope's been hit by a train and put out of our misery.*

"I suppose you're right," Jonny said, lifting a strip of bacon between his fingers. He dipped it into the opaque yellow pool, swished it around a little, then took a crispy bite. "You should call this *The Sordid Tale of Cassidy, Hughes, and Cameron.*"

"Trent would want it named something like *Trent's Big Swole Package,*" Jared said and they both laughed.

"It's always all about him, isn't it?" Jonny said jokingly. "Hell, it'd probably leap off the shelves with a name like that, though."

"Yeah, you're probably right. Some guys have all the luck."

"Oh, he'd be sharing those royalties…"

"… else I'd beat the change right out of his coin purse," Jared said and the two erupted into howls of laughter. If Trent had been home, they'd surely have woken him.

The chuckles continued for a while, then faded into silence. Eventually, Jared got up to take his plate to the sink. Rinsing it, he placed it into the dishwasher.

"You finished my man?"

"Huh? Oh!" Jonny said, slumping over his plate. "No, not yet. I'm still picking at it."

"Okay, let me know if you want me to finish it off," Jared said, returning to his chair with a glass of water. "I need to eat a lot today if I'm going to be working out with the two of you."

Coupled with the loud *thud* Jared's ass made as he dropped into the chair, those words felt like a sudden punch in the gut. Jonny jolted himself upright.

"W-what was that?"

"Um, you need plenty of energy when you lift," Jared said coolly. "That comes from eating, unless you're a walking stimulant like Trent."

"I… I know that." Jonny said, unavoidably considering his smaller arms. "But, I'm confused by what you just said."

"With the two of you?"

"Yes."

"It *was* an invitation earlier, right?"

"So, you're saying that you're in?" Jonny asked, feeling queasy.

Jared nodded, but this time it was a bit hesitant.

"In for *all* of it?"

"Yes!" Jared snapped, breath sputtering after. "Unless you keep asking me damn questions. Look, I'll do it, but only if what you said about Trent doing anything to make *you* happy is true."

"I think it is," Jonny said. "He seemed genuine about it. As much as Trent can seem genuine about anything that's not in his best interest."

That was enough for Jared; he knew Trent well enough.

"Okay then," Jared said. "I'm in this for *you*, Jonny. As such, Trent is going to have to play second fiddle if this is going to work."

Oh boy, he's not going to like that at all, Jonny thought.

"You think he's going to go along with that?"

"He has to, doesn't he?" Jared replied. "What was it he told you to say to me? 'We need to make sacrifices?'"

"Yeah, he did say that, but his sacrifice was apparently inviting you to Swole in the first place. I don't know if he's going to want to follow *your* lead."

Jared notched his shoulders back, then jerked his head to the left. There was a soft *pop* in his neck and a look of relief fell across his face.

"Oh, that's not what I meant at all," he replied. "You see, if I'm going to do this then Casanova Cassidy is going to play second fiddle to the both of us."

"What are you talking about?" Jonny asked, a little confused.

"A proposition of my own," Jared said, smiling. "I'm talking about the man in the middle…"

CHAPTER 3

THREE'S COMPANY

S URPRISINGLY, WHEN JONNY MESSAGED
TRENT over social media later that morning, he was
agreeable about the conditions Jared placed on the night. For some reason,
Jonny was expecting more of a protest, but the only question Trent had for
him was: "Will that make you happy?"

Jonny wasn't about to look a gift horse in the mouth, quickly
telling Trent yes. A few seconds later, a single thumbs-up emoji popped up

on the screen, along with instructions to meet at Sir Mixalot at eight thirty.

Looks like things are definitely a go then, Jonny thought, though he couldn't really believe it.

He sent the confirmation to Jared, who would be away until just after noon visiting his friend Greg (the same guy who had told them about the overlook where they'd picnicked earlier in the week). Apparently, Greg lived in one of the fraternity houses on campus and wasn't feeling well after the weekend. With the other fraternity brothers out doing their own thing, Jared agreed to run by the pharmacy to get him some medication.

Jonny was impressed by Jared's willingness to help those who needed it, wishing he was there to massage his aching shoulder. Turning, he looked over to his right one, rubbing it as if to apologize.

"Well my friend," he told it softly before wincing from a sudden lick of pain. "I have no idea what's about to happen, but if this week has been anything to go by, you're in for a brutal session."

IT WAS TWENTY PAST EIGHT and Jared's Maserati glided into the parking lot of the Summerset Center, avoiding the potholes Trent seemed to target with ease.

Jonny was in the passenger seat, perched as far forward as he could get. Trying to stave off a torrent of sweat, he was sure the leather seat beneath his gym shorts was already suffering.

Ahead and to the left of the windshield, speckled with drops from a brief evening shower, Swole's red neon light burned brightly, calling as it always did the closer Jonny got to the strip mall.

This time, Jared veered right, cutting diagonally across the parking lot.

Jonny looked further down the line of stores. Past the clothing store which bordered Swole on the right, there were a few mom and pop eateries, then a comic book store named Heroes Never Die, then a nail salon, and at the very end, in a colorful kaleidoscope of colors, was Sir Mixalot.

"What exactly is that place?" Jonny asked, pondering their sign. It was a smiling unicorn holding a large cup in one neon configuration, switching to one that was vomiting a rainbow in the other.

"It's a smoothie joint," Jared replied. "Can't you tell?"

"No, not right off," Jonny said, peeking inside where he saw a gaudy arrangement of menus mounted on bright orange walls.

There were swirls of slushies –green, blue, red, purple, and yellow – behind banks of fresh ingredients that could make a wide variety of flavors when thrown into the blender. There was also a single, large man wearing the smallest black tank and shorts that the kids section of any good clothing store could stock.

"There's Trent, looking douchey as ever," Jared said as the car stopped. He switched it off and opened the door. "The place's décor could be toned down a notch, but I used to come here all the time when I worked out at Swole. Greg does too after work; he's at the comic book store just down there past the nail salon. The drinks here are actually really good."

"Where do you work out now?" Jonny asked as he got out of the car. It just dawned on him that he'd never seen Jared lift a single weight.

"I just use the campus gym now."

"Isn't that place shitty?"

"Yes, if you're comparing it to Swole, but it gets the job done," Jared said. Both car doors slammed and the duo made their way for the store. "All I have to do is move heavy things and eat. My body responds well enough."

"That's nice…" Jonny said, his teeth clamped tight in a smile. What he was really thinking was: *Fuck off, you lucky bastard.*

Jared was first to reach the door, his outstretched arm awash in color as it grabbed the handle. He held it open, letting Jonny go in first.

"Oh lord, all the studs are coming tonight," said the wisp of a man behind the counter.

He was fanning his flushed face with both hands and his uniform was splattered with colors. At first Jonny thought they were stains, but upon closer inspection they were there by design. The bright and vulgar look was topped off by a tiny purple hat with an even tinier unicorn horn jutting from the top.

"That'll be later," Trent said smugly, turning toward Jared and Jonny. The former was in his old gym gear; non-stylish, black and white, but functional. The latter was wearing the same outfit he'd worn on chest day, recently washed. Trent could smell the fabric softener as he got close.

"Whatever you say, T-bag," Jared scoffed, talking to the menu instead of Trent.

Jonny giggled, but stopped short when he heard when Trent grunt.

"I can definitely tea bag ya too, J-rod," Trent snipped. "Just like old times."

The worker coughed lightly as if to let them know he was still there. His face had grown even more red from the recent exchange. His eyes were bulging, but Jonny couldn't tell if they were due to fear or lust.

"C-can I h-help you gentlemen?"

"Yeah," Trent said, still looking at Jared. "I'll take a large banana cream, plus one whole banana to go. I'll also buy whatever these two want."

"Oh my," said the clerk.

Jonny shot his eyes sideways toward Trent. *A banana? What the hell does he have…*

"I'll take a cucumber mint," said Jared suddenly, "along with one whole *cucumber* to go."

"Ohhhhh my," the clerk repeated, hands flapping wildly. They sounded like bird wings beating the air. "What size?"

"Large," Jared said, giving the clerk a brief wink.

Trent chuckled, swiping a hand through his hair. Jared did the same and they both looked in Jonny's direction.

So many options, and colors, and flavors.

"I… think…" Jared stammered. "I'm just going to stick with vanilla. M-medium, please."

"Well, okay then," said the clerk, mildly disappointed but after looking toward Trent he performed a monstrous gulp and shot his eyes right back at Jonny. "No extra long fruits or vegetables for you tonight?"

Jonny shook his head, afraid to look. His back was dripping with sweat and his ears burned red like the gym's sign.

"Alrighty, I'll get started on these right away. It should all be ready in about five minutes or so minutes."

With that, the clerk sped away, returning a short time later with a banana and cucumber in hand. He set them down gingerly on the counter, then left again. Jonny could hear him muttering about muscles and being close to fainting, but the sound of blades crushing ice soon took over when things got *really* interesting and he could no longer make out what was being said.

Jonny risked a peek at his companions. Both Trent and Jared had already made it to the counter, grabbing hold of their respective items. Then, they looked at him with smiles so huge they were almost predatory.

"What do you plan to do with those?" Jonny asked.

"You'll find out," Trent told him.

"Yes, you will," said Jared, but he was not looking toward Jonny at all.

"Vanilla," said the clerk, resting a Styrofoam cup on the counter. The smiling unicorn was on it. "Cucumber Mint and Banana Cream," he said a minute later, setting down two huge cups. The vomiting unicorn was on these.

"Hey that's not fair," Jonny said, snatching his cup off the counter. "Those are so much bigger."

Trent shrugged, grabbing his smoothie before plunging a red plastic straw into it. Cream rose around the hole, frothy and light. Grabbing the tip of it, Trent raised it up and down slowly and it made a subtle squeaking noise like old springs on a worn mattress.

"Smallest cup for the smallest dude," he said. "Be back, I'm going to pay for these."

Jared was the last to get his drink. He took a sip and found it was light and refreshing.

"Wanna sip?" he asked Jonny, who was chugging away on his but looked like he needed something more refreshing.

"No thanks," Jonny said, waving him off. He almost got brain freeze. "I'm just fine with this, because I'm sure tonight is going to be the furthest thing from vanilla I can expect."

"You're right about that," Trent said as he returned.

He walked right up beside Jonny and wrapped a large arm around him, nearly ripping the shirt. Pulling Jonny close, he sucked hard on the straw.

Jonny could smell cologne as Trent leaned in toward his ear, whispering, "you wish that I was sucking you like that right now?"

Nervously, Jonny looked over to Jared, who was still standing a couple of feet away. He glanced over to Trent, whose emerald eyes were so close to his.

"Yes, I do."

"Well, you won't have to wait long. Neither will beer can boy." He raised his voice. "Come on J-rod, let's bounce. Swole closes up in about fifteen; we can get to work right after that."

TRENT AND JONNY WALKED BENEATH the shopping center canopy on their way back to Swole. Jonny was getting even more uneasy the closer they got to the gym. He did his best to hide it, but his body language was telling all his secrets while every sound was amplified – from their footsteps, to Jared's car engine as he pulled his car around to park next to Trent's, to Trent madly sucking that creamy smoothie like there was no tomorrow.

"You okay?" Trent asked in his typical gruff tone.

"Yeah, I'm fine," Jonny said unconvincingly.

"You *sure* about that?"

Jonny shook his head, taking a tiny sip. Maybe he should have gotten something more exotic to spice up his mood. They made aphrodisiac smoothies, right?

"I'm not sure about anything right now."

"No need to fret, Jonny-boy, it's not the end of the world. You know that the both of us are doing this because you said it makes you happy, right?"

Jonny stopped briefly, dizzy for a second, then resumed.

"You and Jared both seem fascinated with me being happy," he said.

"Duh."

"Well I can't for the life of me figure out *why* either of you would be so invested."

Trent walked a few paces (they were more self-assured strides than normal steps) and then looped the fingers of his free hand around the straps dangling in front of Jonny's shorts.

"Stop overthinking things, Jonny-boy. I'm sure J-rod has his reasons, but for me it's because you're just *you*, man. I can't explain it any better than that." He sighed briefly. "You remember me telling you that most of my fuck buddies are the slam, bam, thank you ma'am variety?"

"Yeah," Jonny said. "All of them."

"All of them but one. There's something different about you that I haven't felt in a while."

"From Jared?" Jonny asked, causing Trent to laugh loudly.

"So, he told you then? About us?"

Jonny took another swig of vanilla, nodding.

"Well shit. That takes a little bit of the edge off my attitude, doesn't it?"

"No," Jonny said, "quite the opposite for me. It seems that ever since I found out about you two, I feel closer to you than before. Both of you. I don't really understand what that means right now."

"It means you're some kind of man-glue, Jonny-boy, and that takes talent, or better put, someone that can just love and be real without so many goddamn trappings that end up strangling the life out of a relationship."

"Agreed, though I'm not so sure I like the man-glue part."

"Jesus you're whiny. First you don't like being called a 'buddy' when I meet you."

"Still don't," Jonny added with a smirk.

"And now," Trent pressed on, "I'm pouring my heart out and you don't like being called man-glue. What's wrong with you?"

They both chuckled enthusiastically.

"I think you just answered your own question about why we like you," Trent said. "You bring something to us that neither could do alone. Shit, not sure if I fully like the idea, but you're turning into an integral part of my… our lives. Kind of like triple drop sets: hate doing them but in the end, you're better off."

Jonny didn't say it outright, but he felt the same. His conversations today confirmed Trent and Jared both got something from him (in turn, he also thought, something that formed a bridge between them). In turn, he received what he needed from each of them.

"There you go again with your personal training lingo," Jonny said lightheartedly.

"Hey, I tolerate your nerd speak."

"Oh, trust me, I wasn't complaining," Jonny replied, grabbing the hand Trent was leading him with. He guided it toward his crotch, where Jonny's hard dick was waiting.

"Here's Jonny!" Trent said in a pretty good Jack Nicholson voice. Then he squeezed, causing Jonny to squint.

"Jared can see us, you know," Jonny said, a staggered breath puffing out of his open mouth.

"Let him," Trent said. "He'll be better for it, too."

Jonny smiled. Trent released his hold.

"I appreciate everything you've done for me this week."

"Me too Jonny-boy. I can't lie: this guy will be missing your ass when you go home." Trent was pointing right at his dick (again), which always seemed to be semi-hard but right then it was straining against the baby-sized shorts he had on.

"Aww, I'm going to miss him too," Jonny said. "More than the dumb thing he's attached to."

"Keep talking shit like that and you'll regret it," Trent said softly. "Besides, look. We're here and you're about to get it… really good."

Jonny gulped, looked up and to the right, and saw the familiar interior of Swole come into view.

CHAPTER 4

SPIT ROAST

J ONNY COULDN'T SEE ANYONE INSIDE, unlike the night before when those two envious women wrapping up their cardio stared daggers at him just for walking behind Trent. Then he recalled the massive man Will, wrapping up his behemoth leg routine. What stood out most in his mind as Trent opened the door was Will's legs. They were so full of blood, the skin sinewy and taut with veins the size of tree roots, crisscrossing down the entire length. It was quite disgusting to look at, but oh so incredibly hot to stare.

"Come on boyo," Trent called, holding the door open for Jonny who was still mulling over Will's legs in his mind.

Snapping to, Jonny rushed over and grabbed the handle, waiting for Jared to lumber over with his gym bag.

Trent was already heading back toward the lockers when he spun around, walking backwards.

"You remember the layout?" Trent yelled to Jared.

"Yeah," he replied, shutting the door. "I even remember the alarm code."

"What if I changed it? It has been a while since…"

"You wouldn't be able to remember it if you did," Jared cut in insensitively. "The place clear?"

"Seems to be," Trent answered, taking a last look in the rooms as he passed. "You can go ahead and set it."

"Already done," Jared said.

Walking up to Jonny, he grabbed his hand, holding it all the way back to the locker room.

"You ready for this?" he asked gently, the tone offering the chance for escape should he want or need one.

"Yeah, I think I am now," Jonny replied, his face alight with happiness.

"Good stuff!" Jared said, pleased.

Pushing the wooden door of the locker room, the duo entered and nearly collided with Trent. He was standing next to the lockers, one arm braced against the blue metal as he changed into some roomier clothes.

"I figured you'd keep the child attire on," Jared said, setting his bag down on one of the benches. Rummaging around inside, he took out a container of pre-workout and held it out to Jonny. "Want some?"

"Sure," Jonny replied, grabbing the black tub. Moving over to the sink, he unscrewed the lid, dug around for the scoop, and took a heaping serving. A few seconds later, he was back and handed the container over to Jared. "Thanks."

"Welcome," Jared said, using a thumb to lovingly wipe away some of stray powder that had collected on Jonny's upper lip and chin. Then he winked at him. "Damn you're messy."

"That he is," Trent cut in, "and regarding my clothes, I normally would keep that outfit on, but let's be honest. Who am I trying to impress here? Jonny already knows I'm the better of the two."

Jared rolled his eyes again.

"Really?" he asked, taking a scoop of pre-workout for himself.

"You bet your plump ass I am," Trent retorted.

Jared collected some water from the sink in his palm, then chugged it. After he swallowed, he walked back over to his gym bag, put the container inside, and zipped it up.

"It's because I squat more than you."

"As if," Trent said.

"Oh God, please don't whip your dicks out again," Jonny said in a wavering, helpless voice.

"Delts," Trent replied, not unaware of what Jonny had said.

Jonny shuddered looking at the size of both men's shoulders.

"No worries, J," Jared said reassuringly. "I normally go light on shoulder day. The need to go heavy is sort of a myth, unless you're a gigantic bodybuilder."

"Well tonight we'll be doing triple drop sets," Trent said.

"Triple?" Jared said. "Suddenly normal drop sets aren't good enough for you?"

"No, they're just fine, it's just with the three of us here I was *trying* to be charming for this special occasion."

"By subjecting Jonny's shoulders to that amount of burning? Very polite."

"Guys, I'll be okay," Jonny said, his feeble voice somehow cutting through the fog of testosterone leeching out of the two men.

They both turned their heads, looking right at Jonny. Bright blue and green eyes tunneled into him and every magnificent line, curve, and crevice was augmented ten times by the overhead lights.

Suddenly, Jonny didn't feel as okay as he had just second ago, reaching a point where he wondered if he would make it through the workout alive.

THE LOUDNESS OF JONNY'S FINAL grunt during that last set of seated shoulder presses was sufficient to send chills down both Jared and Trent's backs. All of them were sweltering, their clothes dark and drenched with sweat and cologne.

Trent and Jared had both spent the entire workout trying to outdo each other (yet still making sure Jonny was continuing proper form for his sets). The result was a tremendous skin-splitting pump that had them all swollen larger than life.

Jonny lowered his arms then let the dumbbells drop to the spongy mat. He was wiped out, unable to hold them anymore.

"I'll get those," Jared said, picking up the fifteen pound weights before returning them to the rack.

"Thanks," Jonny said, just as he felt a pair of rough hands rubbing on the base of his neck.

"How's that feel?" Trent asked, answered by a long moan.

Jared dropped to his knees in front of Jonny's bench, working to remove his partner's shorts. As he wriggled the sopping fabric down Jonny's slender thighs, his dick sprung free and was sticking straight up like a lollipop in a candy shop.

"The only thing missing here would be some shiny candy," Jared said, moving in with his tongue primed. He licked the tip gently, tracing the ridges slowly.

"Damn right," Trent said, getting harder much faster than he expected to watching Jared give Jonny a blowjob. He carried on massaging Jonny's neck, asking Jared: "You gonna take it?"

Jared didn't answer with words, only actions. His lips wrapped around Jonny's engorged head, sucking out drops of salty-sweet nectar. He went further down on it, the dick spreading his mouth apart. Before long it had reached the back of his throat and he slowly drew back, each slippery inch revealing itself.

Trent moved his hands onto Jonny's chest, one hand going further down his torso.

Then, Jared's blue eyes twinkled like sapphires in the night, looking right at Trent. They asked him to join, pleading for that to happen.

Who was Trent to argue with a look like that? Whatever would make Jonny happy would make him a happy man indeed.

Standing straight up, Trent peeled off his tank top and shorts, his swinging cock grazing against the back of Jonny's neck as he turned. Walking around to the front, Trent kneeled right beside Jared, where he too started to lick Jonny's dick, starting at the base and working his way up.

Jared was still sucking on the tip, making sure to take his time until Trent was just within reach. Jared pulled back, moving Jonny's dick toward Trent's glistening mouth like a peace offering.

Trent gladly accepted, his beard tickling Jonny's cock as it was sucked fast and hard.

Jonny moaned, the change in pace quickening his heart beat.

"Oh God," he whimpered. "I love you guys…"

Trent felt something; Jared's hand had wrapped around his stiff shaft. It started beating. Trent drew back with a gasp, setting Jonny's cock free for a moment.

Jared latched his other hand around Jonny and started sucking him off again, continuing to beat Trent into submission with his other hand.

"J… I…." Jonny stammered.

Trent leaned forward and started to kiss Jared, Jonny's cock locked in a tantalizing prison between their lips.

"I…"

The two men continued kissing, sucking, and licking… loving every second of it.

"I'm about to cum…" Jonny warned, just before he showed his appreciation with seven spectacular jets of hot cum.

That didn't stop Jared nor Trent, not for a second. They continued torturing Jonny's cock between their lips, his head sensitive and raw. Lapping up what they could from each other's faces and Jonny's shaft, they both stood up when done.

Jonny was breathing heavily, looking down at his dick. It was clean and still rock hard, ready to go again.

"Guys," Jonny said. "Wow. Let me tell you that was –"

Before Jonny was finished, Trent had yanked him up mid-sentence. Leading him over to a flat bench, Trent sat down on it, then laid back as if waiting.

Jared joined them a second later, having taken off his clothes. He kissed Jonny and Jonny stole a feel of his body. It was immense, easily the biggest of the three while his dick was undoubtedly the thickest.

Both Jared and Jonny loomed over Trent, looking down on him as he laid on the bench. His arms were up and behind his head, grabbing the bench tightly. While his legs hung off the sides, his cock standing at full attention.

"So, what do you want to do?" Jared asked Jonny. "Fuck or suck?"

Trent's abs twitched at the question, his arms were tense and veiny.

"I'll have him suck me," Jonny said, looking over to Jared's beer can thick shaft. "Trent said thickness didn't matter, right?"

"You're right," Jared said and his weighty cock throbbed once.

All Trent could do was smile.

"Quit your yapping and bring it, boyos."

Jared moved into position, grabbing Trent's thighs. Lifting them, he scooted underneath, the head of his dick pressing against the cushioned entrance to Trent's ass, buried beneath mounds of muscle.

On the other side, Jonny sat down at the head of the bench and moved himself underneath Trent's arms, positioning his dick right across Trent's forehead. The tip reached down past his nose, hovering gracefully right above his mouth. The mere thought of skull fucking Trent just like he had been (twice) caused him to leak precum onto Trent's upper lip, coating his beard with a thick sheen.

"You ready, baby?" Jared asked.

Jonny nodded, rising slightly and pushing forward. His balls pressed against Trent's face as his dick pushed his lips open, plunging into his warm and wet throat.

Jared spat on his dick, shifting himself up and forward. Trent's ass parted like the sea against the force of Jared's monster, which found his hole seconds later. He tried to push in, but Trent resisted.

Jonny could feel Trent convulsing, the shudders rough and unpredictable. A whimper came, then a painful wince, then a look of incredible calm as his body relaxed. Jared was inside.

Pushing slowly, Jared struggled with himself to not go full blast on this mother fucker's ass. Instead he took it nice and slow, so slow that all Trent could feel was agonizing bliss. Trent's cock had softened slightly from the initial discomfort, but it was leaking so much precum it looked as if he were pissing.

Jonny resumed hammering Trent's skull, wrapping his hands around the man's neck and using that to guide his cock down this throat.

Jared had gotten just shy of halfway, the point where his shaft was thickest and stopped. He looked up, watching Jonny buck and whip his head back and forth as his cock disappeared and reappeared from Trent's mouth.

"Jonny," he called. "I want that."

Jonny looked up while continuing to ram his dick down Trent's throat.

"You want this end?"

"No, I want that action," Jared clarified. "We're going to have to flip him over.

Trent had heard what they were saying and began to withdraw. Jared's hands stopped him.

"Where are you going?" he asked almost callously. "You're staying right where you are.

Jonny understood what they were about to do, and hoped he had enough strength left to do it. Looking down at Trent's instable green eyes, he thought he could muster plenty. Something about Trent being at their mercy drove him on.

It was then that Jared started to stand, still buried in Trent's ass. Jonny rose also, struggling a little to hold onto Trent's bulk, but eventually both were standing upright (even though Jonny's legs were slightly buckled) and they began to spin Trent while he was impaled from both sides. It was a slow, grunt filled trip, but damn was it fun. Weaving over and under oncoming arms and legs the duo started to descend, Trent now face down on Jonny's cock.

"Once you touch that bench," Jared said, "be ready."

Trent was already working Jonny's dick when he felt his stomach touch the bench's soft wrapping.

Jared had slipped out about an inch during the process, giving Trent a little bit of a reprieve. That was about to change.

"Here we go," Jared said, then without another word he shoved his hips forward as hard as his muscular body could move them. The three inches that had been buried inside Trent suddenly became the full eight by eight in the blink of an eye.

Trent cried out in pain, but Jared didn't stop.

He pulled back and rammed himself inside again.

He could feel Trent squirming during each thrust.

He could feel his body begging for him to stop but Trent's dick, sticking out between his bucking legs, was already shooting ropes of jizz. They were striking, like white paint that had been splattered on the black benchtop.

Jonny was the next to go, Trent's beard causing him to lose it. Trent didn't pull back, swallowing every drop that Jonny let go inside his mouth.

With two men spent, Jared was all that was left. He lifted Trent's ass and continued to pound away with pleasurable ease.

Jonny looked up and saw Jared's determined face, sweat flinging from it in every direction.

His breathing was getting faster, a fire building deep in his chest. Letting lose a low growl, Jared pulled out, pushing Trent's ass down and away. Grabbing his sore shaft, it unleashed over a dozen glazed jets, one striking Jonny in the mouth, two on his chest, and the rest coating Trent's rippled back like a honey bun.

Jared stood there for a second, unable to speak.

Trent felt euphoric, so much so that he couldn't move.

Jonny was exhausted, partly saddened they hadn't been doing this since day one.

"*That*, my friends, is what thickness gets you," Jared said at last, collapsing into a mass of sweat and meat on top of Trent.

Jonny couldn't help but laugh at the sight; both men looked like they could fall asleep at any moment.

"We may have to take a nap before heading home," he said. "You all look dreadful."

"Speak for yourself, Jonny-boy," Trent mumbled, his face pressed against the bench.

"It's actually not that bad of an idea," said Jared.

"Oh, let me go prepare the bedrooms," Trent said bitterly. "You think this is a hotel?"

"No, it's a brothel," Jonny said and Jared joined him in laughter.

"Whatever," Trent said. "If I was able to move I'd beat the shit out of you…"

"I think we're past the need for that," Jonny said with an air of sadness. "Sad to think we only have one more session before I go home."

"Yeah," Trent said somberly.

"Right," Jared said. "Plus, it's sad to think I've been missing out on this."

"Y'all had your own brand of fun though," Trent said.

"True," Jared said.

"Hey," Jonny said with a sudden burst of energy. "What were you planning to do with the food?"

"Huh?" Trent and Jared said in unison.

"The banana and the cucumber…"

"Dude!" Trent said with his last bit of energy. "I was going to *eat it*. Geez. Not *everything* has to be sexual."

"Yeah, but I thought…"

It was too late, Trent was snoring and Jared held up a single finger to his lips.

Wriggling free, Jared walked over toward the pile of his clothes and feeling around, pulled out the cucumber which he had placed in his pocket earlier.

Jonny also wormed himself loose, stepping away because whatever Jared had planned was not going to be pretty.

"I was never planning to eat mine," Jared said as he creeped back up behind Trent. He looked across to Jonny. "You better be prepared to run."

"Oh God, Jared, what are you up to?"

Jared smirked devilishly, holding the cucumber close to Trent's ass with one hand, the other hovering over the end. Then, he reared the free hand back before bringing it down with force in a single arcing motion.

THE END

ABOUT THE AUTHOR

In the beginning, Golden worked the standard corporate rat race, completing college with a chemical engineering degree before starting a small photography company on the side.

Since then, the FuriousFotog brand grew into an internationally recognized brand, published in both domestic and international magazines, on websites, and trade/e-book book covers (even appearing on some himself).

Having been in the industry since 2012, Golden has interfaced and networked with countless other authors, clients, and photographers to license and create over 400 romance book cover images, diversifying into commercial work as well.

He published his debut novel, Homeward Bound (Journeyman 1) in June 2016, completing the six-book series in January 2017.

Websites:
http://www.goldenczermak.com/
http://www.onefuriousfotog.com/
Facebook:
http://www.facebook.com/authorgoldenczermak
http://www.facebook.com/furiousfotog
Newsletter:
https://goo.gl/ZoLqC4

Made in the USA
Middletown, DE
25 July 2017